MW00902265

Published in 2007 by Concordia Publishing House
3558 S. Jefferson Avenue, St. Louis, MO 63118-3968
1-800-325-3040 • www.cph.org

Manufactured in China

1 2 3 4 5 6 7 8 9 10   16 15 14 13 12 11 10 09 08 07

That Easter Morn

Art by
Chi Chung

CONCORDIA PUBLISHING HOUSE • SAINT LOUIS

Alleluia

O sons and daughters of the King,
Whom heav'nly hosts in glory sing,
Today the grave has lost its sting!

Alleluia!

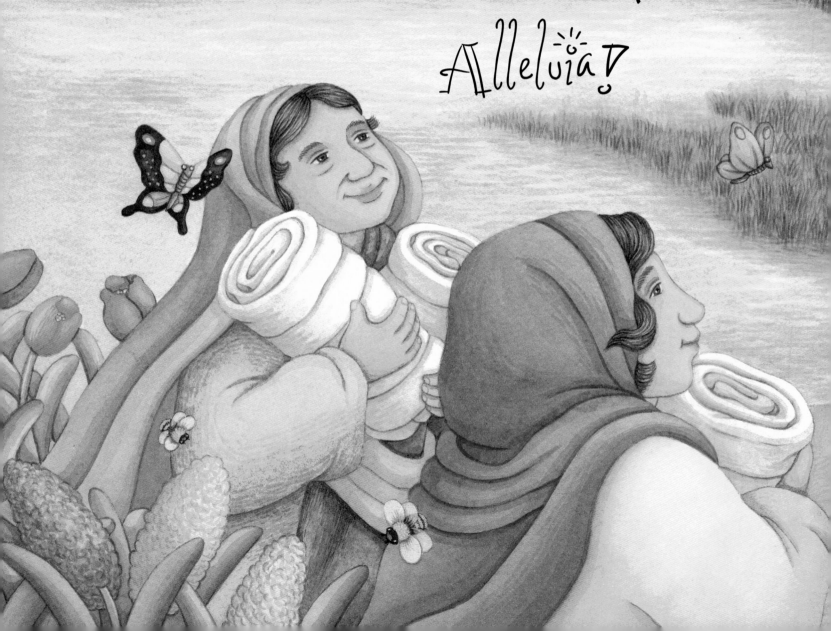

That Easter morn, at break of day,
The faithful women went their way
To seek the tomb where Jesus lay.

Alleluia!

An angel clad in white they see,
Who sits and speaks unto the three,
"Your Lord will go to Galilee."

Alleluia!

Then Mary in the Garden cried.
But then before her very eyes,
Her Savior spoke, "Yes, it is I!"

Alleluia!

That night the apostles met in fear;
Among them came their master dear
And said, "My peace be with you here."

Alleluia!

When Thomas first the tidings heard
That they had seen the risen Lord,
He doubted the disciples' word.

Alleluia!

"My wounded side, O Thomas, see,
And look upon My hands, My feet;
Not faithless but believing be."

Alleluia!

No longer Thomas then denied;
He saw the feet, the hands, the side;
"You are my Lord and God!" he cried.

Alleluia!

How blest are they who have not seen
And yet whose faith has constant been,
For they eternal life shall win.

Alleluia!

On this most holy day of days
Be laud and jubilee and praise:
To God your hearts and voices raise.

Alleluia!

Alleluia

O Sons and Daughters of the King

Refrain

Al - le - lu - ia, al - le - lu - ia, al - le - lu - ia!

1 O sons and daugh - ters of the King,
2 That Eas - ter morn, at break of day,
3 An an - gel clad in white they see,
4 That night the a - pos - tles met in fear;
5 When Thom - as first the tid - ings heard

Whom heav'n - ly hosts in glo - ry sing, To - day the
The faith - ful wom - en went their way To seek the
Who sits and speaks un - to the three, "Your Lord will
A - mong them came their mas - ter dear And said, "My
That they had seen the ris - en Lord, He doubt - ed

grave has lost its sting! Al - le - lu - ia!
tomb where Je - sus lay. Al - le - lu - ia!
go to Gal - i - lee." Al - le - lu - ia!
peace be with you here." Al - le - lu - ia!
the dis - ci - ples' word. Al - le - lu - ia!

6 "My piercèd side, O Thomas, see,
And look upon My hands, My feet;
Not faithless but believing be."
    Alleluia!

7 No longer Thomas then denied;
He saw the feet, the hands, the side;
"You are my Lord and God!" he cried.
    Alleluia!

8 How blest are they who have not seen
And yet whose faith has constant been,
For they eternal life shall win.
    Alleluia!

9 On this most holy day of days
Be laud and jubilee and praise:
To God your hearts and voices raise.
    Alleluia! *Refrain*

Text: attr. Jean Tisserand, d. 1494;
tr. John Mason Neale, 1818–66
Tune: O FILII ET FILIAE, French, 15th cent.

Text and tune: Public domain